BUG PATROL

by Denise Dowling Mortensen • Illustrated by Cece Bell

Clarion Books • Houghton Mifflin Harcourt • Boston   New York   2013

Clarion Books • 215 Park Avenue South, New York, New York 10003

For information about permission to reproduce selections from this book, write to

Permissions, Houghton Mifflin Harcourt Publishing Company, 215 Park Avenue South, New York, New York 10003.

Clarion Books is an imprint of Houghton Mifflin Harcourt Publishing Company. • www.hmhbooks.com

The illustrations were executed in acrylics and ink. • The text was set in Chaloops. • Book design by Sharismar Rodriguez.

Library of Congress Cataloging-in-Publication Data • Mortensen, Denise Dowling

Bug patrol / by Denise Dowling Mortensen ; illustrated by Cece Bell. • p. cm.

Summary: Captain Bob of the Bug Patrol keeps a watchful eye on bugs everywhere. • ISBN 978-0-618-79024-1 (hardcover)

[1. Stories in rhyme. 2. Insects — Fiction. 3. Police — Fiction.] I. Bell, Cece, ill. II. Title. • PZ8.3.M842Bug 2013 • [E]—dc23 • 2011041586

Manufactured in China • LEO 10 9 8 7 6 5 4 3 2 1 • 4500389716

To my brothers and sisters—
Ellen, Skip, Sean, Patrick, Maura, Linh
—D.D.M.

For Jerry Kalback and Doug Goldsmith,
and for Eric May, wherever you are
—C.B.

WEE-O! WEE-O! WEE-O! WOO!

Bug Mobile coming through!

Write an
accident report.
Hand out tickets.
Tempers short.

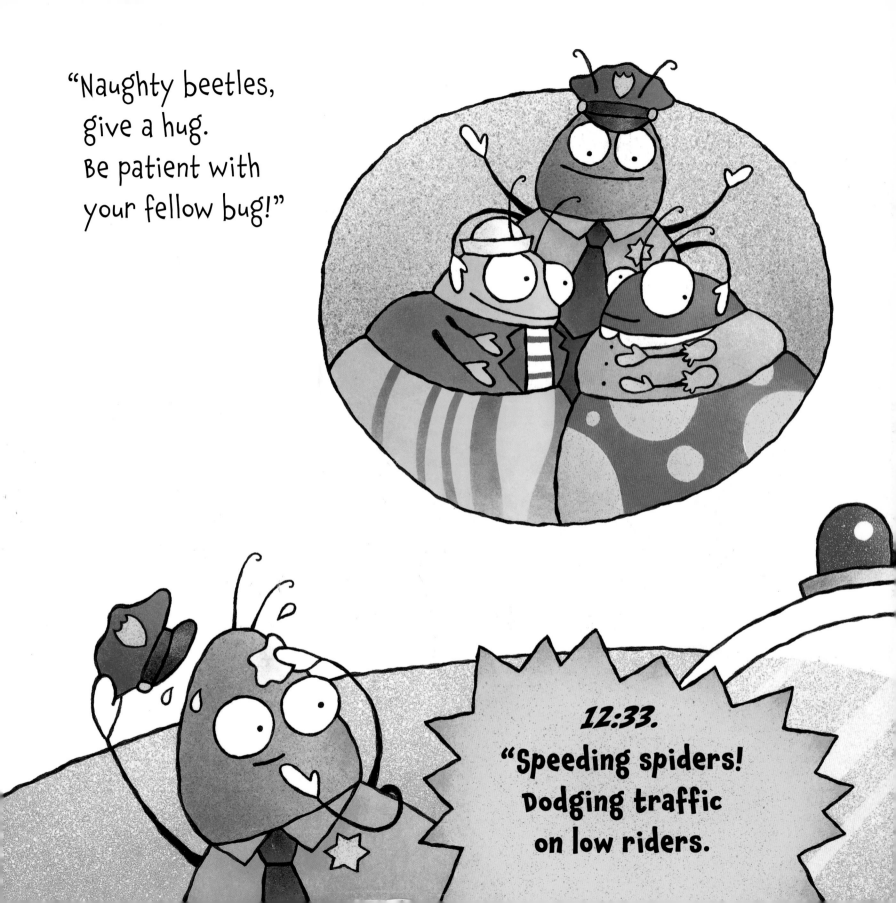

Corner spiders
in an alley.
End of motorcycle
rally.

Perpetrators
lectured, fined.
No more speeding.
Peace of mind.

Grab a wrap.
Walk my beat.

Wave hello.
Shoot the breeze.
Catch up with
the local bees.

3:15.
"Sidewalk swell.
Picket line
at Roach Hotel.

Take those roaches
for a ride,
to a place
more dignified.

Where food is
free and homes
are nice.
"Behold—
the Landfill Paradise!"

4:53. "Emergency!
Report of mother
missing flea.

Use my
magnifying glass.
Find that flea
in the grass.

Cradle him
in my palm.
Keep him safe.
Call his mom.

Doggie, Mom,
and her flea.
Reunited.
Happily.

7:48.
"Investigate:
Party crickets
up too late.

WEE-O!
WEE-O!
WEE-O!
WOO!

Bug Mobile
coming through!

Megaphone
turned up high.
Play my cricket
lullaby.

Hurry home
to my nest.

And the bugs
that I love
BEST!